Nutcracker Night

Mireille Messier
&
Gabrielle Grimard

pajamapress

First published in Canada and the United States in 2019

Text copyright © 2019 Mireille Messier
Illustration copyright © 2019 Gabrielle Grimard
This edition copyright © 2019 Pajama Press Inc.
This is a first edition.

10 9 8 7 6 5 4 3 2 1

www.pajamapress.ca   info@pajamapress.ca

 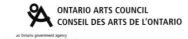

The publisher gratefully acknowledges the support of the Canada Council for the Arts and the
Ontario Arts Council for its publishing program. We acknowledge the financial support of the
Government of Canada through the Canada Book Fund (CBF) for our publishing activities.

Library and Archives Canada Cataloguing in Publication

Title: Nutcracker night / Mireille Messier & Gabrielle Grimard
Names: Messier, Mireille, 1971- author. | Grimard, Gabrielle, illustrator.
Description: Illustrated by Gabrielle Grimard.
Identifiers: Canadiana 2019008698X | ISBN 9781772780918 (hardcover)
Classification: LCC PS8576.E7737 N88 2019 | DDC jC813/.54—dc23

Publisher Cataloging-in-Publication Data (U.S.)

Names: Messier, Mireille, 1971-, author. | Grimard, Gabrielle, illustrator.
Title: Nutcracker Night / by Mireille Messier & Gabrielle Grimard.
Description: Toronto, Ontario Canada : Pajama Press, 2019. | Summary: "In a text full of
onomatopoeia, a small child travels to see the Nutcracker Ballet, describing the experience in a series
of sounds"— Provided by publisher.
Identifiers: ISBN 978-1-77278-091-8 (hardcover)
Subjects: LCSH: Nutcracker (Choreographic work) – Juvenile fiction. | Ballet – Juvenile fiction.
| Sounds (Words for) – Juvenile fiction. | Christmas stories. | BISAC: JUVENILE FICTION /
Holidays & Celebrations / Christmas & Advent. | JUVENILE FICTION / Performing Arts /
Theater & Musicals.
Classification: LCC PZ7.1M477Nu |DDC [E] – dc23

Original art created with watercolor, gouache, oil, colored pencil and digital media
Cover and book design—Rebecca Bender

Manufactured by Qualibre Inc./Print Plus
Printed in China

Pajama Press Inc.
181 Carlaw Ave. Suite 251 Toronto, Ontario Canada, M4M 2S1

Distributed in Canada by UTP Distribution
5201 Dufferin Street Toronto, Ontario Canada, M3H 5T8

Distributed in the U.S. by Ingram Publisher Services
1 Ingram Blvd. La Vergne, TN 37086, USA

To the pitter-patter of little feet in ballet slippers.
May the magic of dance always stay with you!

–M.M.

To my mother Madeleine, who brought
me to see *The Nutcracker* ballet almost
every year of my childhood

–G.G.

Swoosh!
go the cars.

Beep! Beep!

goes our taxi.

Pshhhh!
goes the fancy fountain.

Swish! Swish!
goes my frilly dress.

Clip!
Clop!
Clip!
Clop!
go Daddy's new shoes.

Chitter!
Chatter!
Chitter!
Chatter!
goes the crowd.

–Tickets, please!
says the usher.

Pickle-dee!
Zing!
Boom!
Ding!

goes the orchestra as it tunes up.

Clap!
clap!
clap!
clap!
clap!
goes the audience.

Tick!
Tick!
Tick!
goes the conductor.

Hushhh!

go the parents.

Crinkle-crinkle
goes the tissue paper.

Stomp-stomp!
goes the boy.

Snap!
goes the doll.

Sniff-sniff
goes the girl.

Chrrrick,
chrrrick,

goes the head
as Godfather fixes the doll.

Bong!

Bong!

Bong!

Bong!

Bong!

Bong!

Grrr!
Grrr!
Grrr!

growls the Mouse King.

Shwap! Shwap! Shwap! go the soldiers.

–Ho!　　　–Hurray!

Click!
go the lights.

It's intermission!

Slurp!

Hahaha!

Fizz!

Klink!

Crunch!

Ding!
 Ding!
Ding!

goes the bell.

ZZZZZ...

goes the man in a red scarf.

Takka-takka-takka,
goes the Sugar Plum Fairy.

Zoombando!
go the flamenco dancers.

Shuffle-shuffle!
Jingle-jangle!

go the polichinelles.

Bravo!
Brava!
goes the crowd.

"Did you enjoy the ballet?"
asks my dad.

Smooch!

goes my kiss.

The Nutcracker

is one of the most famous ballets in the world. Russian composer Pyotr Ilyich Tchaikovsky wrote the music. The story is based on stories by E.T. A. Hoffmann and Alexandre Dumas.

The Nutcracker was performed for the first time in 1892 in Saint Petersburg, Russia. The ballet has since become a family classic every December, with hundreds of productions staged around the world. It is often the first ballet children attend, and it is known to have sparked a lifelong love of dance in many young hearts.

The story goes like this: Marie (also known as Clara) and Fritz's parents are having a fancy party on Christmas Eve. The children's godfather arrives with special gifts—a toy for Fritz and a wonderful nutcracker soldier doll for Marie. Fritz is jealous and breaks Marie's doll. The godfather fixes the doll with his handkerchief, but Marie is still worried about her nutcracker. After the party ends and everyone has gone to bed, Marie sneaks back downstairs and falls asleep next to her beloved doll. In Marie's dream, the Christmas tree magically grows. The nutcracker comes to life and becomes the Nutcracker Prince. Toy soldiers become his army as he battles the Mouse King and his army of mice. After the Mouse King is vanquished, the prince takes Marie to the Land of Sweets, where whimsical creatures and characters dance for them.

When she wakes, Marie is at the foot of the Christmas tree, hugging her nutcracker. Was it really just a dream?